Aye, My Eye!

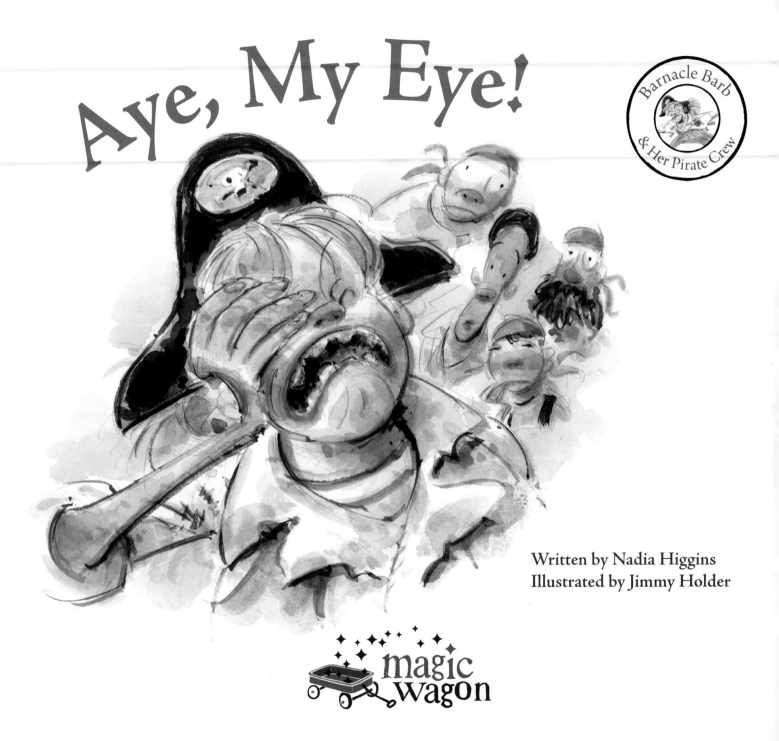

Barnacle Barb
& Her Pirate Crew

Written by Nadia Higgins
Illustrated by Jimmy Holder

magic
wagon

For my sweet, funny Cecilia

visit us at www.abdopublishing.com

Published by Magic Wagon, a division of the ABDO Publishing Group, 8000 West 78th Street, Edina, Minnesota, 55439.

Printed in the United States.

Text by Nadia Higgins
Illustrations by Jimmy Holder
Edited by Bob Temple
Interior layout and design by Emily Love
Cover design by Emily Love

Library of Congress Cataloging-in-Publication Data

Higgins, Nadia.
  Aye, my eye! / Nadia Higgins ; illustrated by Jimmy Holder.
    p. cm. — (Barnacle Barb & her pirate crew)
  ISBN 978-1-60270-090-1
  [1. Pirates—Fiction. 2. Birthdays—Fiction.] I. Holder, Jimmy, ill. II. Title.
PZ7.H5349558Ay 2008
[E]—dc22

                      2007036971

Barnacle Barb's cries rang out over the high seas.

"Arrrrr-arr-arrr-arrrgh! Arrrrrr-arr-arrr-arrrgh!"

She wailed. She bellowed. She blubbered like a whale.

"Now, now, Barrrb," said Armpit Arnie, as he patted his friend's dusty shoulder. "It's your birthday. You should be dancing a jig, not carrying on so! What's got you so undone?"

"Me heart's been snapped like a piece of driftwood!" Barb moaned. "And all because of that scurvy dog, Pegleg Pedro."

"Pegleg?" Armpit Arnie exclaimed. "But he's no scurvy dog. He's your best friend!"

"Not anymore," Barb declared. "Here it is almost nightfall and that scumfish hasn't even wished me 'Happy Birthday'! Just wait until I find him. He'll be walking the plank, that ungrateful, one-legged scallywag!"

"Poor Barrrb," Arnie said to himself. He thought for a minute. "Aha! I know just the thing to cheer her up."

Arnie called all the other pirates to the upper deck. "Stinkin' Jim! Slimebeard! Shrimp-Breath Sherman! Ahoy, maties! Barnacle Barrrb needs our help!"

"Now listen here," Armpit Arnie said. "Barnacle Barrrb's got the birthday blues. And I know just the game to cheer her up."

"Hammer the Hammerhead!" the group called out together.

"You guessed it, me hearties!" Arnie said.

The crew worked fast to set up the game. Shrimp-Breath pinned up the poster of the hammerhead shark. Stinkin' Jim pulled out the bag of hammers.

Slimebeard got Barb and told her the good news.

"Aw," Barb said, wiping a brown smear across her face. "If only that lobstersnot Pegleg Pedro were half as considerate as you dear mates."

Arnie went first. With all his force, he threw a hammer at the hammerhead. But the hammer missed. "Arrrgh," Armpit Arnie sighed.

Shrimp-Breath threw next. His hammer managed to graze one of the hammerhead's fins. "Two points," Arnie called out.

Slimebeard threw a six-pointer. Then, Stinkin' Jim's hammer got tangled up in a fishnet.

Finally, it was Barb's turn. "Watch and learn," Barb said as she picked up her enormous hammer. "One, two, three, heave!" *Smack!* It hit the hammerhead right between the eyes, making a gash right through the poster.

The pirates whooped and hollered. "Barb threw a slasher!" they cheered.

Shrimp-Breath Sherman picked up Barb on his shoulders for a victory dance. "You're 108, and you're still great!" the pirates chanted.

Arnie threw handfuls of bait like confetti. Stinkin' Jim scattered all the gold coins from his pocket. Then Slimebeard started juggling the hammers . . .

"AAAAAAAAYYYEEEEEEE!" Barb shouted.

"Aye! Aye! Aye!" the other pirates shouted.

"Not 'Aye!,' ye daft squidbait!" Barb screamed. "AAAAAAYYYYEEEEEE, my eye! Your hammer bonked me head," Barb shrieked. "Me eye! It popped out!"

There it was. Barb's glass eye sailed across the deck in a slow, graceful arc.

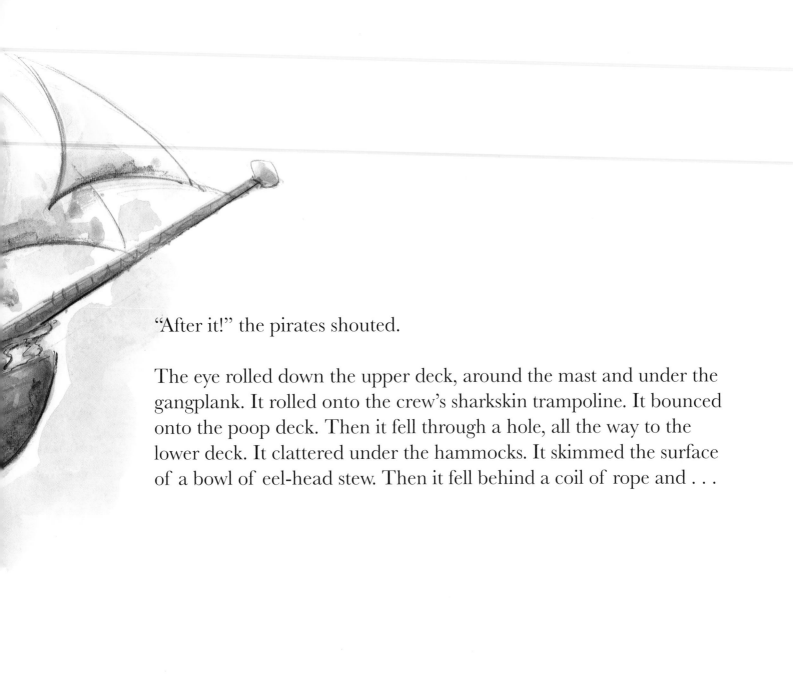

"After it!" the pirates shouted.

The eye rolled down the upper deck, around the mast and under the gangplank. It rolled onto the crew's sharkskin trampoline. It bounced onto the poop deck. Then it fell through a hole, all the way to the lower deck. It clattered under the hammocks. It skimmed the surface of a bowl of eel-head stew. Then it fell behind a coil of rope and . . .

"Arrrrr-arr-arr-arrrgh! Arrrrrr-arr-arrr-arrrgh!" Covering the hole where her eye used to be, Barb wailed. She bellowed. She blubbered like a whale.

"We lost it, maties," Barb moaned. "That eye cost me 600 doubloons worth of stolen treasure," she sighed. "Arrrrgh, Billy," she said to her parrot, "go fetch me eye patch."

The pirates trudged back to the upper deck.

"Another game of Hammerhead, Barrrb?" Stinkin' Jim offered.

"'Tis no use, Stinkin'," Barb said. "This has got to be the worst birthday in history—even for a 108-year-old pirate."

Meanwhile, down in the hold, Pegleg Pedro was wondering what all that noise was overhead. "How am I supposed to concentrate with all those worthless wobbegongs making such a ruckus?" he huffed.

He held his magnifying glass back up to his good eye and got back to work. Here it was, almost nightfall, and he still hadn't finished making his best friend's birthday present.

Once again, Pegleg examined all the jewels spilling out of the open treasure chest. He ran the sparkling gems through his dirty, sausage-like fingers.

"Arrrgh. 'Tis no use," he said at last. "I'll not be finding the perfect jewel to finish Barrrb's birthday necklace," he sighed. He picked an ordinary ruby from the pile. "This'll have to do," he said.

But then, just as Pegleg Pedro leaned over to put away his magnifying glass, he spied something magnificent by his feet.

"It's a beauty!" Pegleg gasped. He picked up a sparkling green orb, turning it in his fingers. "Why didn't I see it before?" he wondered.

Quickly, Pegleg added the prized gem to Barb's birthday necklace. He scampered to the upper deck.

"Yo-ho-ho and a happy birthday to you, Barrrb," he called out.
"Barrrb?" he looked for his friend. Then he saw her.

"Shiver me timbers, Barrrb! You look terrible—even for a pirate!
And why are you wearing that old eye patch again?" he asked.

"'Tis a long story, you crab-hearted scoundrel," Barb said.

"Oh, but I have something to cheer you up," Pegleg retorted.

"No more Hammer the Hammerhead!" Barb shouted.

"What?" Pegleg Pedro said, pulling his closed hands from behind his back. "No, no, Barrrb. Just close your eyes—I mean, eye—and count to three."

"Arrrrgh, okay," Barb said. "One. Two. Three."

Barb opened her eye.

"Aye!" Barb screamed. "My eye!"

Barb tore the glass eye off her birthday necklace.

"My necklace!" Pegleg Pedro wailed as the broken necklace scattered around the deck.

Barb popped her eye back into her head. "What necklace?" she asked, blinking. "Who would give a pirate a necklace for her birthday?" she laughed.

"Oh, Pegleg, you are a jokester," Barb said. She put her old friend in a headlock.

"You found me eye, my little love-lubber," Barb said,
"and if I weren't a pirate, I'd kiss you!"

Pirate Booty

- Did female pirates really exist? A few did. Anne Bonny and Mary Read disguised themselves as men to join a pirate crew. A Chinese woman, Cheng I Soa, was even a pirate captain. She sailed the South China Sea in the early 1800s, leading a fleet of 2,000 ships. This fierce swashbuckler is said to have paid her crew a reward for every enemy head they brought to her.

- Pirates did wear earrings, but they didn't consider the earrings jewelry. They believed earrings helped prevent sea sickness by pressing on one's earlobes.

- People have used "glass eyes" since the late 1500s. The first glass eyes were curved pieces of glass or shells that were tucked behind the eyelids. They were sharp and uncomfortable. Round, smooth glass eyes first came into use in the mid-1800s.

Pirate Translations

ahoy, maties — hello, friends
avast — stop
aye — ouch, or yes
doubloon — pirate money (a Spanish gold coin)
me hearties — my friends
scallywag — rascal
scurvy dog — scoundrel
shiver me timbers — oh, my
yo-ho-ho — hi